Groundwood Books / House of Anansi Press
groundwoodbooks.com

We gratefully acknowledge the Government of Canada for its
financial support of our publishing program.

With the participation of the Government of Canada
Avec la participation du gouvernement du Canada | Canadä

Library and Archives Canada Cataloguing in Publication

Title: The Homesick Club / Libby Martinez ; pictures by Rebecca
Gibbon.
Names: Martinez, Libby, author. | Gibbon, Rebecca, illustrator.
Identifiers: Canadiana (print) 20190153431 | Canadiana (ebook)
2019015344X | ISBN 9781773061641 (hardcover) | ISBN
9781773061658 (EPUB) | ISBN 9781773063546 (Kindle)
Classification: LCC PZ7.M36828 Ho 2020 | DDC j813/.6—dc23

The illustrations were done in acrylic ink, gouache and colored
pencils on acid-free cartridge paper.
Design by Michael Solomon
Printed and bound in Malaysia

To my family, who never
stopped believing in me.
And to everyone around the
world who is a member of
the Homesick Club. — LM

For my sister Sarah. — RG

The Homesick Club

Libby Martinez

Pictures by Rebecca Gibbon

Groundwood Books
House of Anansi Press
Toronto Berkeley

"Mónica," whispers Hannah. "Where is Mrs.
Jackson?"

Principal Rivera is standing in front of our
class with a lady I've never seen before.

"Class," says Principal Rivera. "Mrs. Jackson
had her baby on Saturday. This is your new
teacher, Miss Shelby."

Hannah and I look at each other.

"New teacher!" I whisper.

$$5-1=4$$
$$4+1=$$
$$2+3=$$
$$8-6=$$

"It is sooooo nice to meet you, class," says Miss Shelby. Her voice is soft and slow, like her words are stuck together with syrup.

Miss Shelby tells us that she is from Texas.

She says this is the first time she has lived in a city full of skyscrapers.

We laugh when she tells us about her first trip on the subway.

Texas is far away. I am from Bolivia, even farther away.

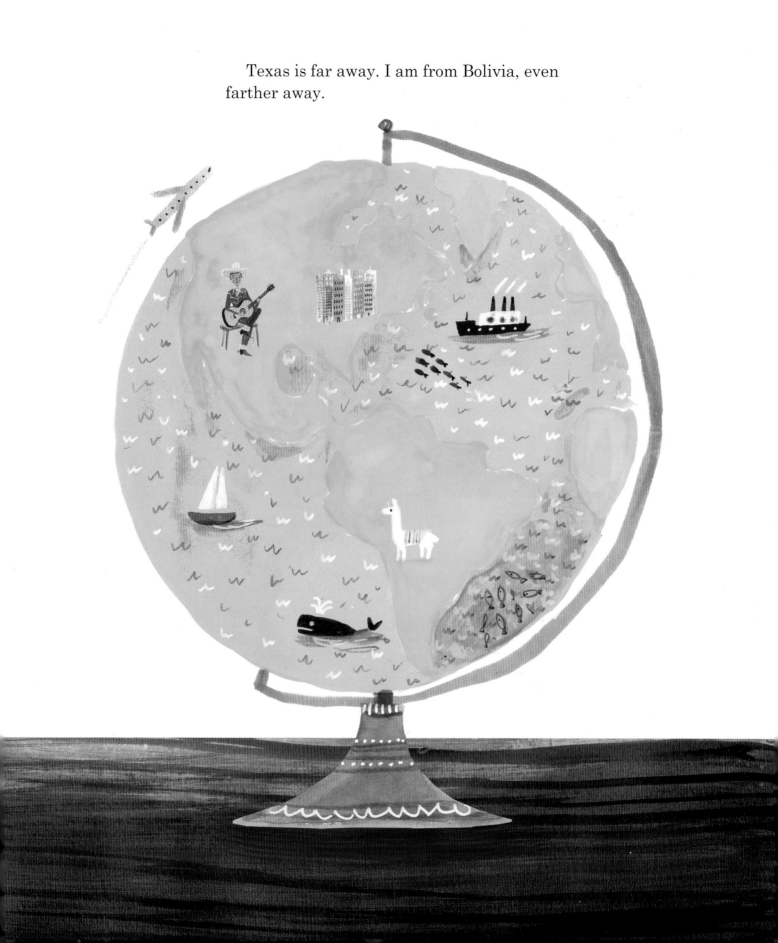

In Bolivia, there are lots of mango trees and green vines. A family of hummingbirds — *una familia de colibrís* — lived in our backyard. My grandmother and I fed them sugar water every morning.

Hannah is from far away, too. She is from Israel. She says it's always sunny there, not like here where the sun hides all winter.

She brought photos to Show and Tell — pictures of giant sand dunes and a tiny tortoise that lived near her house.

My day for Show and Tell is Friday.
I wish I could bring a hummingbird,
but I've never seen one here. I think
all of the honking and noise probably
scares them away.

Mrs. Jackson told Miss Shelby that we are learning all about the stars. Miss Shelby tells us about the Big Dipper and Orion the Hunter.

"Where I lived in Texas," she says, "the sky was sooooo big and wide you could see the shapes of animals in the stars."

The sky was big and wide in Bolivia, too. Sometimes I tried to count all of the stars. It's hard to see the stars here because of the tall buildings and bright lights. I wonder if Miss Shelby misses the stars like I do.

After science, we have lunch in the cafeteria. Hannah and I always sit together. We are the Homesick Club because we miss where we used to live. We made a special sign with a picture of a hummingbird and a tortoise.

"I miss hearing frogs go
croak-croak at night," I say.
Hannah laughs.

"I miss hearing the wind," she says.
"In the desert, it goes *whoooooooo*, like
a whistle."

Miss Shelby is standing by herself in the cafeteria. All of the other teachers are standing together and talking. It's hard to be new, even if you are a teacher.

On Tuesday, Miss Shelby teaches us about the sun and the moon. My grandmother still lives in Bolivia, but we both see the same moon at night. Some people wish on stars, but I wish on the moon — *la luna*. Last night, I wished for something to take to Show and Tell on Friday.

"Maybe we should ask Miss Shelby to be part of our club?" I whisper to Hannah at lunch. "She is from far away, too."

"Mónica!" whispers Hannah. "Miss Shelby is a teacher!"

I look at Miss Shelby and then back at Hannah.

"I'm going to ask her," I say.

I walk over and stand by
Miss Shelby. She smells like
flowers and summer.
"Miss Shelby, would you
like to be part of our club?"

Miss Shelby smiles and looks over at Hannah and our sign.

"Can you tell me about the Homesick Club?" she asks.

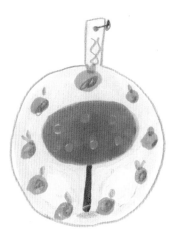

"You have to be from far away," I say. "I'm from Bolivia and Hannah is from Israel. We talk about things we miss. Do you miss all the stars you could see in Texas?"

"Yes," she says. "I miss seeing all of those stars. I would love to join your club, Mónica."

Miss Shelby sits down at our table and tells us about other things she misses.

"I miss peach trees," she says. "I miss the raccoon that used to peek through my kitchen window at night.

"And I miss hummingbird cake."

"Hummingbird cake!" I say.

"Don't worry, Mónica," she says, laughing softly. "It's only called hummingbird cake because it is sooooo sweet, like the flowers that hummingbirds drink from. It's the best cake in the whole wide world."

I tell Miss Shelby about the hummingbirds that lived in my backyard in Bolivia. I think I have an idea for Show and Tell. I am going to ask my mom to help me.

After school on Thursday, my mom and I go to the grocery store on the corner. We buy bananas, pecans, cinnamon and a can of pineapple. My mom lets me stir all the ingredients together in a big bowl. We watch my secret rise in the oven. When it's cool, we spread the thick cream cheese frosting.

"Mónica, are you ready for Show and Tell?" Miss
Shelby asks the next morning.

I walk very slowly to the front of the class because
I don't want to drop my surprise.

"I brought a hummingbird cake," I say.

Some of the kids giggle, but I tell them it's Miss Shelby's favorite cake in the whole wide world. I tell them about the hummingbirds that my grandmother and I fed in Bolivia.

"It's hard to move far away," I say.

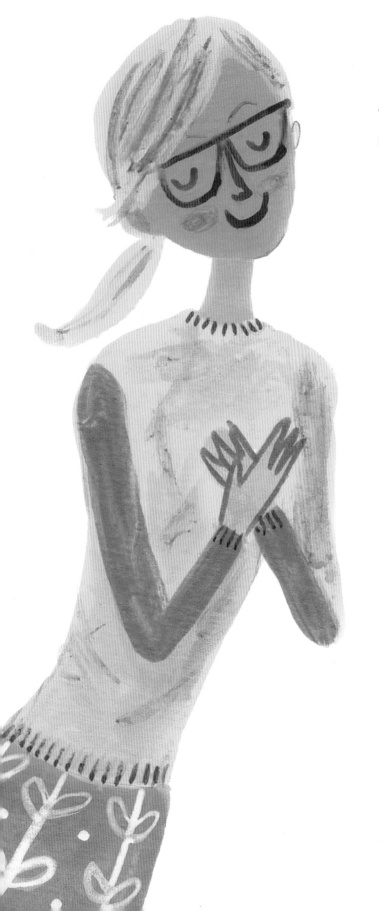

Miss Shelby comes and stands beside me. She closes her eyes and smells the cinnamon-y sweetness.

"Home," she says. She blinks and blinks.

At lunch, Hannah and I watch Miss Shelby. She is talking with one of the other teachers. She smiles when she sees the new picture that Hannah drew on our sign.

Miss Shelby will always be part of the Homesick Club.

Homesick Club

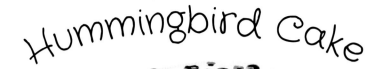

Hummingbird Cake

Cake

3 cups all-purpose flour
1 cup granulated sugar
½ cup brown sugar
1 teaspoon salt
1 teaspoon baking soda
2 teaspoons ground
  cinnamon
½ teaspoon ground nutmeg
  (optional)
1 cup vegetable oil
3 large eggs
2 cups mashed bananas
1 cup crushed pineapple,
  undrained
2 teaspoons vanilla extract
1 cup chopped pecans and
  a handful for decorating
  (nuts optional)

Frosting

2 (8 oz.) packages cream
  cheese, softened
1 cup butter, softened
5 cups powdered sugar
2 teaspoons vanilla extract

Ask an adult to help you with these steps.

Preheat the oven to 350°F. Lightly butter and flour three 9-inch round cake pans.

In a large bowl, whisk together the flour, sugar, salt, baking soda, cinnamon and nutmeg. Add the oil, eggs, bananas, pineapple, vanilla and pecans. Stir everything together.

Divide the batter evenly among the three cake pans. Bake for 25 – 30 minutes until the top springs back when gently pressed in the middle. Remove the pans from the oven and let cool completely.

To make the frosting, use a mixer to beat the cream cheese and butter until smooth. Add the powdered sugar and vanilla while beating at low speed. Increase speed to high and beat frosting for 2 minutes.

Remove the cakes from the pans. Place one cake layer on a platter and cover with frosting. Place the second layer on top and cover with frosting. Place the third layer on top. Spread the remaining frosting over the top and sides of the cake. Sprinkle chopped pecans on top.